D0010053

Curr
PZ
7
.m86
Fr
1995

From Far Away

by Robert Munsch and Saoussan Askar
illustrated by Michael Martchenko

Annick Press
Toronto • New York

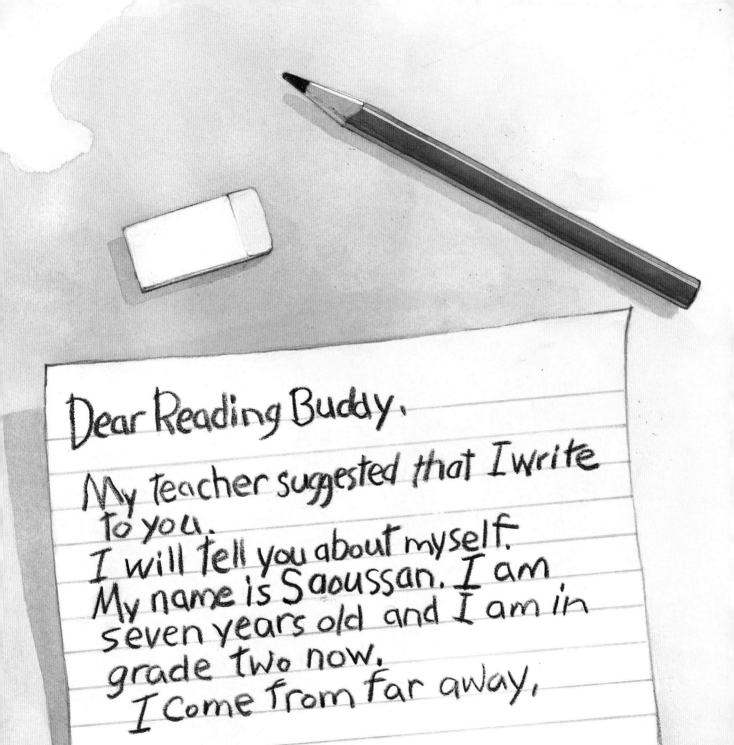

Dear Reading Buddy,

My teacher suggested that I write to you.
I will tell you about myself.
My name is Saoussan. I am seven years old and I am in grade two now.
I come from far away,

The place we used to live was very nice, but then a war started. Even where my sister and I slept there were holes in the wall. Finally, one day, there was a big boom and part of our roof fell in. My father and mother said, "There is no food and we are getting shot at. We have to leave."

My father left and was gone for a long time. Then a letter came with plane tickets to Canada.

I did not know anything about Canada, but the next day I was on a plane going there. As soon as the plane moved I got sick. I stayed sick for the whole trip, which was two days long. I didn't like it. Nobody wanted to sit near me.

Once we got to Canada, my father took me to a school and left me there, after he showed me the girls' bathroom. He said, "Be good and listen to your teacher."

So I was good and I listened to my teacher, only I didn't know what she was saying because she did not know how to talk right. So I just sat and listened. Children were trying to talk to me, but I was not able to answer them because I didn't speak English.

When I wanted to go to the washroom I didn't know how to say, "I want to go to the washroom." That's why I used to crawl to the door when the teacher turned her head and looked at the other side of the room. When someone opened the door I crawled out and went to the washroom. When I came back from the washroom, I waited beside the door. When someone opened the door I crawled back in and went to my desk.

Once I crawled to the washroom and saw a Hallowe'en skeleton, only I did not know what Hallowe'en was. I thought the skeleton was evil. I thought that people were going to start shooting each other here. I screamed a very good scream:

Aaaa ahh hhhh hhh hh!

Everybody came running out of the rooms. They thought someone was being killed in the bathroom. My teacher opened the washroom door and tried to tell me that it was Hallowe'en time and the skeleton is paper.

I didn't understand her and I didn't know what Hallowe'en was. She jumped up and down and danced around to explain to me that Hallowe'en is just fun, but I thought the skeleton made her crazy and I screamed louder:

Aaaa ahh hhhh hhh hh!

Then she hugged me to make me feel better. I felt as if my mother was hugging me. I jumped on her lap and pee went down my knees because I was scared to death. That happened so fast, and I felt guilty and ashamed of myself and I didn't know how to say, "I am sorry." But the big tear that went out of my eye said it for me.

Then I went and sat by the front door of the school till my father came and got me. I had decided that the whole school was crazy and I did not want to stay there.

When my father came, he told me about Hallowe'en, and said that people here are not going to start shooting each other.

I had bad dreams about skeletons for a long time after that, but finally I began to talk, little by little. I learned enough English to make friends, and school started to be fun. Now I am in grade two/three and I am the best reader and speller in the class. I read and write a lot of stories. The teacher is now complaining that I never shut up.

This year when it was Hallowe'en I wore a mask and we had a party at school. Then I went with my sister trick-or-treating to the neighbours'. We got candy and nobody shot at us the whole time.

I decided that Canada is a nice place, and I changed my name from Saoussan to Susan, but my mother told me to change it back.

The kindergarten teacher moved from our school, but sometimes when I see her in the mall I run to her and hug her and wish she was still my teacher. She was my first teacher in Senior Kindergarten and she helped me a lot.

But she still does not let me sit on her lap.

Goodbye,

©1995 Bob Munsch Enterprises (text)
©1995 Saoussan Askar (text)
©1995 Michael Martchenko (art)
Cover design by Sheryl Shapiro

Annick Press Ltd.
All rights reserved. No part of this work covered by the copyrights
hereon may be reproduced or used in any form or by any means
– graphic, electronic, or mechanical – without the prior written
permission of the publisher.

Annick Press gratefully acknowledges the support of the
Canada Council and the Ontario Arts Council.

Canadian Cataloguing in Publication Data

Munsch, Robert N., 1945-
  From far away

ISBN 1-55037-397-8 (bound) ISBN 1-55037-396-X (pbk.)

1. Askar, Saoussan - Juvenile fiction.
I. Askar, Saoussan. II. Martchenko, Michael.
III. Title.

PS8576.U575F7 1995   jC813'.54   C95-931189-0
PZ7.M85Fr 1995

The art in this book was rendered in watercolours.
The text was typeset in Bookman.

Distributed in Canada by: Published in the U.S.A. by Annick Press (U.S.) Ltd.
Firefly Books Ltd.   Distributed in the U.S.A. by:
250 Sparks Avenue   Firefly Books (U.S.) Inc.
Willowdale, ON   P.O. Box 1338
M2H 2S4   Ellicott Station
                                 Buffalo, NY 14205

Printed and bound in Canada by
Metropole Litho Inc., Montréal, Québéc.

CURRICULUM LIBRARY